NAKED YOGA

AN EROTIC ADVENTURE

VICTORIA RUSH

COPYRIGHT

Naked Yoga © 2018 Victoria Rush

Cover Design © 2018 PhotoMaras

All Rights Reserved

OTHER BOOKS BY VICTORIA RUSH:

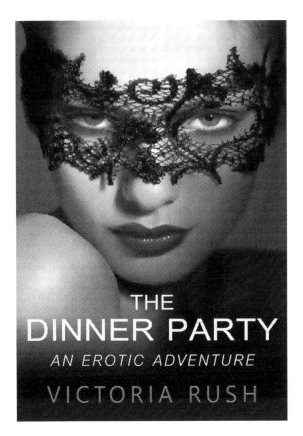

Everyone's an exhibitionist in disguise...

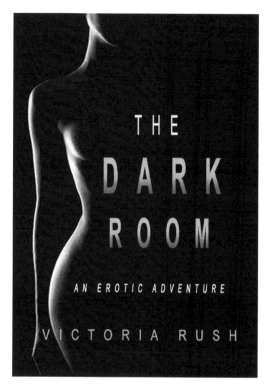

THE DARK ROOM

AN EROTIC ADVENTURE

VICTORIA RUSH

Everything's sexier in the dark...

For the uninhibited...

1

MIND AND BODY

I'd always enjoyed yoga. There was something about the simplicity of it that appealed to me. No weights, no fancy equipment, just me stretching my own body to tone and relax my muscles. For sixty minutes every day, I had my own island of tranquility on my little yoga mat.

But it was more than that. It was the *sharing* of the experience with like-minded people in the quiet, serene comfort of a yoga studio. Listening to the breathing of my fellow yogis as they stretched and relaxed their bodies inches away from me. For the longest time, I never found anything sexual about the practice. We were just focused on connecting with our own bodies and freeing our minds of extraneous thoughts.

But my recent encounters at the dinner party and in the dark room had given me a new appreciation for the female form. Most of the participants in my advanced class were women, longstanding members with exquisitely toned bodies. And they all wore tight spandex leggings and tops that hugged every curve and valley of their figures.

For some reason, in today's class I was far more interested in focusing on what *other* people were doing than channeling my own chakra. As I transitioned from one pose to another, I couldn't help looking out the corner of my eye at the women surrounding me while they spread their legs and arched their bodies in ever more suggestive poses.

When the instructor asked us to move into the plank position, I stole furtive glances at the women facing me, as their breasts clenched tightly together between their outstretched arms. When we did lunges, I peeked between their legs to see if I could detect the outline of their labia in their tights. When we did the wide-angle forward bend, I ground my pussy into my mat trying to stimulate my tingling love button. And when we moved into the plow position, I fantasized about crouching over their upturned asses and rubbing our pussies together like Emma and I had done in the dark room.

The instructor's gentle exhortations were a blur in the background as my mind raced with lascivious thoughts. I'm sure she would have disapproved of my breaking the cardinal rule of yoga, which was to free your mind and let the distractions of the day melt away. But in my case, something else was melting. The more turned on I got, the more aware I became of the growing wet spot between my legs. I couldn't stop imagining all the positions I wanted to get into with my yoga partners. When we moved into the bridge position and thrust our hips upwards, all I could think about was fucking someone—anyone—as I ground my mound against an imaginary partner.

The more I thought about it, the more excited I got. I began to undress the women with my eyes, imagining what they'd look like doing their poses in the buff. Occasionally, I'd catch some of them stealing glances in my direction.

Were they having the same fantasies as me?

When the instructor guided us into the wide-leg balance position, where we spread our legs and grasped our elevated toes, I thought I was going to faint. So many beautiful women were opening themselves up to me, daring me not to stare at the joint between their legs. I had to will my body to stay in place as I mimicked their pose. My glutes wanted to crawl like a sand crab across the floor until our bodies touched, pressing our pussies and breasts together.

By this time, the wet spot between my legs had grown completely out of control. I could no longer pretend that it was just sweat running down my legs or my ass from the tension of holding the poses. I excused myself and gathered my mat, holding it in front of me as I walked toward the women's change room. When I got into the locker room, I went into one of the stalls and quickly closed the door behind me. I lowered my tights and began jilling my clit furiously, trying to stifle my moans in case anyone else entered the room. It didn't take more than a minute for me to come hard, as I hunched over and stood panting, my back leaning against the stall door.

After I collected myself, I grabbed a towel and headed into a shower stall. I turned on the warm spray from the overhead faucet and felt the water trickle over my tender breasts. As my nipples hardened, I reflected back on what had happened in the yoga studio. I unconsciously bent over into a downward dog pose and felt the stream spray on my exposed ass and pussy. The feeling of being naked, imagining myself performing my yoga pose as other women watched me was electrifying. Within seconds, I had another powerful orgasm as I held my ankles, shaking in convulsions.

Ten minutes later, after I'd changed into street clothes and other women began filtering into the change room, I noticed one of them glance at me with a knowing smile.

Maybe I wasn't the only one who harbored this fantasy of naked yoga, I thought.

I resolved to investigate the idea further when I got home...

2

MASTER OF MY DESTINY

As soon as I got home after work that day, I sat down in front of my computer. The fantasy I'd envisioned at the yoga studio earlier in the day had awakened a yearning for me to go further—to explore how far I could take the concept of uniting my mind and body to experience true enlightenment. Except in my case, the enlightenment I was seeking had more to do with a *sexual* awakening than one of mind or spirit.

If yoga was all about being captains of our own ships so we could learn to be the best versions of ourselves, it was time for me to take matters into my own hands. I opened the Google search box and typed in the words 'naked yoga'. Much to my surprise and delight, I got three hits. The first two were discussion groups between people who enjoyed practicing yoga alone in the buff, talking about how liberating and relaxing they found it to be. But the third result had a short description of a studio that held 'tantric yoga' sessions.

I clicked on the link and the page opened with pictures of beautiful men and women posing stark naked in familiar yoga positions. Their bodies were turned in such a fashion that their genitals were hidden, but their naked buttocks and chests left little to the imagination. A text block below the images talked about the benefits of practicing yoga in the nude and how it freed our minds and spirits to focus on *every* aspect of our physicality. It cited a study that said yoga improves sexual desire, arousal, lubrication, orgasm, and sexual satisfaction. And it talked about how tantric techniques could be used to prolong and elevate sexual pleasure.

But the rest of the website was shy on details as to what these so-called tantric techniques involved and how they were put into practice within the sessions. There were only two other links on the page —one to schedule a session and another simply marked 'Contact'. I clicked the Contact link and it offered three options: Phone, Email, or Chat. I didn't feel comfortable yet talking with someone over the phone, so I clicked the Chat link.

A chat window opened and someone named Soraya began typing in the chat box.

'Hi, I'm Soraya,' she said. 'How can I help you?'

I panicked for a moment, realizing I hadn't actually prepared to talk with someone yet about such a personal subject.

'I'm looking for more information about your naked yoga classes,' I tentatively typed.

'Sure,' Soraya said. 'What would you like to know?'

Geez, I thought. *How can I put this delicately?*

I didn't want to be too blunt, but I didn't want to be too opaque either. I needed more information about their service, but I didn't want to be too presumptive.

I'll just go slow and see what they reveal.

'How many people typically attend your classes?' I began.

'It varies from session to session,' Soraya replied, 'but we normally get between ten and twenty.'

'Is it open to all ages and genders?'

'Our classes are open to men, women, and transgender individuals over the age of eighteen.'

Transgender individuals? That could be interesting.

'Is clothing optional?' I asked.

'We start every session with a disrobing ceremony, where participants are asked to remove their garments. The absence of clothes weaves together naturalist and yogic practices that aims to bring about increased freedom, intimacy, and relaxation.'

Now for the tough question.

'Are session participants encouraged to interact with one another?'

'We have three levels of classes,' Soraya replied. 'Each new member is encouraged to start at the beginning level and step through to the advanced level as they become more comfortable. The level of involvement with other participants increases at each level.'

'What happens at the beginning level?'

'The first level, *Meditation*, is all about getting in touch with one's own body and experiencing the freedom of yoga unencumbered by any outside trappings. This is where you learn to explore and revel in the sensations of your own body by practicing the various asanas in the nude.'

Revel in the sensations of one's own body. I like the sound of that. But I was hoping for more.

'When do we begin to engage our partners?' I asked.

'The second level, *Namaste*, is where you choose a partner and help one another stretch and hold poses. This is where you learn to respect the divinity of your partner while guiding them to expand their horizons.'

Respect their divinity, indeed. I wondered just how far this 'helping' would be allowed to go.

'And the third level?'

'The most advanced level, *Harmony*, is where you seek maximum enlightenment through the joining of your minds, bodies, and spirits. This is where you explore each other's bodies and learn to experience their full potential. It is a deeply intimate bond that our practitioners find most empowering.'

All this spiritual double-talk was dancing around the main subject. It was time to cut to the chase.

'Are we allowed to—' I hesitated for a moment trying to frame the right words. '*Touch* each other?'

'Of course,' Soraya replied. 'This is the whole goal. To release your inhibitions and connect with one another in such a way as to experience maximum pleasure and fulfillment.'

Now we're talking.

Soraya was beginning to sound more and more like an instructor herself, and my mind began to imagine what she'd look like leading us through the poses in the nude. I could feel the blood rushing to my pussy as my insides began to moisten. I was feeling bolder and decided to probe a little further.

'What are these 'tantric techniques' that your website talks about using in the sessions?'

'The word tantric comes from the Sanskrit root tan,' Soraya instructed, 'which refers to the interweaving of threads on a loom. In the context of yoga, it means the joining of partners and using the principles of meditation and relaxation to elevate and prolong one's pleasure. It can be practiced at any stage in your progression through the levels but is most powerful when practiced in tandem with your partner at the most advanced level.'

That sounds exactly like what I'm looking for.

Now it was just a matter of testing the boundaries.

'How can I ensure my privacy and personal space will be respected if I choose not to engage a partner?'

'We establish clear ground rules at the outset of each session. Everyone chooses their own partner and engages only with explicit consent. If you wish to practice your asanas alone, we encourage you to do so. Our time together is always safe, nourishing, and judgement free.'

I was beginning to feel more relaxed and was almost ready to book my first session.

'Do I need to bring anything with me?' I asked.

'All you need to bring is an open mind, a free spirit, and a clean yoga mat. Everything else, including your cell phone and any other electronic devices, we ask you to check at the door.'

I'm all in, I thought.

'When is your next beginner session?'

'Meditation sessions are scheduled Mondays, Thursdays, and

Saturdays, between 7:00 and 8:00 p.m. You can check availability and book a session by clicking on the Appointments tab at the top of the page. Did you have any further questions?'

I didn't really have any other questions, but I was intrigued to learn more about this mysterious Soraya. She seemed a lot more informed about the art of yoga than your typical customer support agent.

'No, thank you for your time and candor, Soraya,' I typed. 'I'm looking forward to participating in your sessions. Are you an instructor yourself?'

'Yes, I'm one of three certified yoginis at our practice.'

'Are they all female?' I wondered. I wasn't sure about the idea of having a male instructor staring at me as I stretched and bent over entirely naked.

'Yes, although depending on your preferences, I think you'll find the male yogis can be just as fulfilling in the practice of tantric yoga as the women are.'

'Thank you, Soraya,' I said. 'I hope to meet you at one of the sessions. I'll book an appointment soon. Bye for now.'

I clicked out of the chat window and tapped on the Appointments tab. I selected the first available date for a Meditation session and quickly filled in my profile and credit card information to pay for all three levels of the naked yoga sessions. Then I stripped off my clothes and placed my favorite vibrating dildo facing straight up on the floor. I placed my straight arms in front of me then pulled my legs behind my shoulders and lifted my ass into a Firefly position above the dildo. As I lowered my pussy onto the dildo, I closed my eyes and imagined it was my yoga partner instead.

Namaste, I muttered, as my breathing began to quicken.

3

MEDITATION

When I got to the naked yoga studio on my appointment day, I was pleasantly surprised. The room was bright, clean, and well-appointed, with tasteful prints on the wall, clean white sheers covering the windows, and a new hardwood floor. This wasn't some dingy pseudo-massage parlor operation as I'd feared.

I arrived ten minutes early, around the time other patrons were beginning to stream in. There was a mix of men and women in their twenties and thirties. Some of them appeared to be couples, judging by the intimacy of their hushed conversations and how close they huddled together. Before long, everybody staked out a spot on the floor and began stretching quietly on their mats.

At first, I was surprised to see everybody dressed in familiar yoga attire. But then I remembered what Soraya had said in our online chat conversation about everybody being asked to disrobe at the start of each session. I placed my purse and coat on a bench in a conspicuous place where I could keep an eye on it, then found an open spot on the floor and began stretching. I wasn't really interested in stretching yet, but it kept me busy and avoiding awkward glances with the people sitting around me.

During a transition in one of my stretches, I looked up and locked eyes with a pretty red-haired girl stretching beside me who couldn't have been much beyond her teens. She was wearing pink tights and a yellow top that pressed against her small but perky breasts. She didn't appear to be wearing a sports bra, and I could see the outline of her nipples as they pushed against soft cotton. We smiled at one another then returned to our stretching as we pretended to ignore the palpable tension in the room.

Shortly after, an attractive woman wearing matching Lululemon tops and bottoms walked toward the front of the room, where she placed a mat in front of the floor-to-ceiling mirrors lining the wall. She nodded and smiled at a few familiar faces, then looked at the large clock on the side wall. It was 7:00 p.m.

"Good evening, everyone," she said, addressing the room. "For those of you who are visiting us for the first time, welcome to our Tantric Yoga program, Level One — Meditations. For those of you who are returning, it's great to see you again. Remember that your progression through the levels should be at your leisure. You should step up to the next level only when you feel comfortable enough with the exercises and with your interaction with your fellow participants."

I wondered if she was Soraya from my chat session. My eyes ran up and down her body, analyzing ever contour of her perfectly shaped figure. Her legs were long and slim and bulging in all the right places. I marveled at the diamond shape of her calves and the line flexing up the side of her tights that separated her gently curved quadricep and hamstring muscles. Her Madonna-toned arms were slender and cut, and I could see the outline of her tricep muscles as she moved her arms. Her stomach was flat as a washboard, and her ample breasts swelled over the top of her tight-fitting top, above a tapering waist. She had a perfect athletic gymnast's figure, and I hoped she'd turn around for a moment to reveal an ass that I was sure I could bounce a coin off.

She was absolutely gorgeous, and I couldn't take my eyes off her. She had a vaguely European look, with dark brown hair, high cheek-bones, and full rosebud lips. As I watched her talk, I imagined pressing my body against hers, kissing her in a passionate embrace. I couldn't wait for the program to start and see her gorgeous body in the buff.

As if reading my mind, she looked at me and smiled.

"My name's Alexandra," she said. "I'll be your instructor for today's session. Shall we get started?"

Everybody including me nodded.

"Our first order of business is to shed the trappings of modern civilization by dispensing with our clothes. These are just holding us back from truly connecting with our bodies and reaching our full potential. Yoga is intended to free our minds, bodies, and spirits. Practicing our craft in the nude will enable us to open our minds and experience true freedom and relaxation. Let's all disrobe now and place our garments on the floor beside your mats."

Alexandra reached over her shoulders and pulled her top over her head then bent over in a perfect pike position and pulled down her yoga pants. Then she nonchalantly stepped out of them and placed them in a neatly folded pile near the mirrors. I hesitated for a moment, soaking up her gorgeous body. Her B-cup tits stood proud and tall on her chiseled chest, with a thin indentation running down the front of her abdomen to her perfectly bald pubis.

When she turned around and bent over to place her clothes on the floor, I gasped out loud. Her ass was as tight and round as a schoolgirl's. The muscles in her glutes flexed as she stretched and contracted them from the bending motion. When she turned back around, I suddenly became aware that I was the only person in the room who was still clothed. I awkwardly pulled my tights off with everybody watching me, then placed them on the floor beside my mat. I could see myself reflected in the mirrors at the front of the room and part of me wanted to move my hands in front of my pussy to cover up. But everyone else seemed perfectly relaxed being naked, and I scanned the expanse of mirrors to take in the sight.

There were about fifteen people in the room, in various shapes and colors. Some had dark bodies, and some had fair skin like me. Most were slim and toned, but there were a few curvy girls with full breasts and wide hips. I noticed two men standing near the back of the pack, and I wondered if they'd chosen this position out of shyness or because it offered the best position for viewing the women's bare backsides. I squinted to see if I could detect any sign of tumescence in their hanging members, but they appeared to be fully relaxed and flaccid. I was glad that they'd also trimmed their bushes short and neat so as not to interfere with maximum viewing pleasure.

"Right, then," Alexandra said. "Now that we're fully free to relax and connect with our bodies, I'd like everyone to lie down on your mats face up and place your arms gently at your side. Close your eyes and breathe in slowly through your nostrils, then exhale deeply to remove the troubles of your day. Try to empty your mind and focus on the beauty and serenity of your body."

It was strange lying on my yoga mat completely naked, knowing I was surrounded by so many people in a similar state of undress. I was tempted to turn my head and open my eyes to steal another glance at Alexandra or the girl beside me, but I followed her instructions and focused on my breathing. It felt liberating to take my clothes off around like-minded strangers, and I could feel myself begin to relax as a cool draft swept over my body. The stillness in the room was a welcome respite from my hectic workday.

After two or three minutes, Alexandra instructed us to open our eyes and sit up on our mats in the Buddha position.

"Cross your legs, bringing your heels under your knees, then lift your chest so your spine is straight. You may open your eyes if you wish, as you can begin to feel comfortable in your natural body among your peers."

I raised my eyelids and turned my head slowly to look around the room. The young girl beside me caught my gaze and looked straight into my eyes. I smiled at her as her eyes drifted down my chest and she looked at my exposed breasts and stomach. I unconsciously lifted my chest and pushed my tits out as far as I could. My breasts were much larger than hers, and I was proud of how firm and high they still stood at my age. I could feel my nipples hardening and I blushed slightly as I glanced at her tight figure.

Her skin was flawlessly smooth and unblemished, and she had barely an ounce of fat anywhere on her body. Her small boobs seemed to be glued onto her chest, as if somebody had sculpted them out of clay. They barely moved as she breathed in and out, rising in tandem with her expanding ribs and diaphragm. Her nipples were small, with pinched areolas betraying her excitement. Maybe it was just the cool air circulating in the room, but her nipples were definitely standing out in an aroused state. I lifted my eyes and we smiled at each other, in tacit approval of each other's physiques.

I frowned when Alexandra interrupted our connection, instructing us to change position.

"Now that we're getting comfortable in our natural bodies," she said, "let's expand our horizons and begin to stretch our capabilities. I'd like you to extend your legs straight in front of you and gently flex your toes toward your knees. Now, gently lean forward with a straight spine and run your hands along the top of your tights toward your feet until you feel some gentle pressure in your hamstrings. Hold the position, breathing slowly and deeply, until you feel your muscles relax, then push forward another inch, trying to move your head as close to your knees as possible."

My flexibility was pretty good from my regular yoga classes, so I was able to get all the way down and I rest my chest on my thighs, clasping my hands around the undersides of my feet. I looked in Alexandra's direction and she nodded approvingly while holding a similar position without any sign of strain in her face. I turned my head and peeked under my outstretched arm at the young girl beside me and she did the same. We both giggled for a moment, then placed our heads back between our knees and concentrated on our poses. I could feel the mat underneath me beginning to moisten between my legs as I began to think about what I'd like to do with her at the next level in our training.

After another three or four minutes, Alexandra instructed us to move into the next position.

"You're all doing wonderfully," she said. "Now we're going to move into a new position to really give those hammies a workout. Bring the sole of your right foot to rest against your left inner thigh. Now, turn and extend your chest over your left knee, holding your left leg or foot to gently pull yourself forward. As before, breathe slowly and hold the position when it begins to bind, then extend yourself forward in small increments as you feel the pressure in your hamstring slowly relax. Go as far as you can without feeling uncomfortable. Your goal is to elongate your muscles and improve your flexibility so you can be ready for whatever tight spots life throws at us in the real world."

I was feeling a tight spot between my legs, and I pressed the heel of my right foot hard against my pussy. This was the first time I'd actively touched myself in the session, and I began to think about what might be in store as I moved to the more advanced classes and begin to interact more closely with other participants. I hoped that the girl to my side with whom I'd made a silent connection would be there so we could partner up and explore our bodies more intimately.

Alexandra instructed us to switch sides and extend our right leg to stretch the opposite hamstring. The girl and I glanced quickly again at each other before we bent down, and I began to fantasize about going down on her. I wiggled my hips against my left heel, trying to increase the friction against my swollen clit. But Alexandra always seemed to interrupt our poses before I could work up enough sustained contact to go very far.

Perhaps this was by design, to create just enough contact with ourselves and others to make us yearn for a stronger connection with our partners. I had to admire the brilliance of their business model. They were building a powerful desire to move on to the next stage. Just as with normal sex, no one in their right mind wanted to stop before achieving the pinnacle of pleasure.

"Okay," Alexandra said, interrupting my thoughts once again. "Now we're going to try a variation on this pose that will help us stretch our ribcages and build our core. Bring your right forearm down to the inside of your right leg and try to grab the inside of your right foot. Then reach up and over your head with your other arm.

Rotate your left palm inward and try to clasp the outer edge of your right foot while rotating your chest inwards and upwards."

A few people near the back of the room grunted and groaned as they tried the awkward maneuver.

"I know," Alexandra said, "this is a tough one. Just go as far as you feel comfortable without feeling undue strain. As always, pause at the moment of tension and breathe deeply. Feel your tummy pushing in and out as you use your diaphragm to breathe from your belly, not your chest. Glance up toward the ceiling to encourage your body to twist as much as you can. When you begin to relax, push a little further and hold."

This time, the girl next to me and I were facing each other directly, only a few feet apart. We looked at each other and giggled again. We were definitely forming a connection as we ran each other's eyes shamelessly down and across each other's bodies, watching the muscles in our stomachs rippling from the tension of the side stretch. We both had our heels in front of our bare crotches, which only added to the titillation of the pose. I tried to will her to pull her foot away to give me a glimpse of her naked pussy, but we remained obedient to Alexandra's instruction.

Just as I was beginning to think the sequence of poses had been carefully staged to reveal only enough of our bodies to our fellow participants to build an unquenchable desire, Alexandra instructed us to sit up and change position once again.

"Now let's focus on another important element of our core strength, which is our lower back. Sit up and place your legs directly in front of you once again, then bend your right leg until your right heel is touching the inside of your left knee. Now reach up with your left arm and twist toward your right side with your right hand on the floor beside you, placing your left elbow on the outside of your elevated knee. You should feel a gentle stretch in your lower back and glutes. Look behind you and find a spot on the wall where you can focus, then gently try to twist your body further in that direction as you trace a line further along the wall toward your right. Hold, breathe, and relax. Then twist a little further, pushing yourself to twist as far as you feel comfortable."

My gaze was averted away from the girl next to me, so I scanned the room behind me. I could see the two men at the back of the room stretching in the seated twist position, looking just as serious and focused as the rest of us. I caught a few people stealing furtive glances at one another, but for the most part everybody seemed lost in the moment concentrating on their poses, seemingly mindless of their naked and exposed positions.

Alexandra asked us to switch and turn to the other side, which gave me an opportunity to scan the other side of the room. I noticed some of the women glancing in my direction and we smiled as we checked out each other's bodies. So far, the experience had been liberating and mildly stimulating, but I was beginning to grow tired with how we'd been covering up our most erogenous parts with the poses Alexandra had led us through.

"Okay," she said, as if reading my mind. "Now we're going to get a little more risqué in our positions and open up our bodies to channel our chi more freely."

She sat up on her mat and extended her legs straight in front of her. Then she slowly spread her legs apart, exposing her bare vulva to the entire room. My breathing quickened and I became mindful of the growing wet spot on my mat. The slit in her pussy beckoned to me as I unconsciously leaned forward.

"We're going to do a wide-angle seated forward bend, which will stretch and strengthen your adductors and pubococcygeus muscle. I want you to spread your legs straight out and as far to the sides in front of you, then lean forward with a straight back as you reach out with your hands toward your outstretched feet. You'll feel a tightness between your legs, so you have to do this slowly and carefully so as not to pull anything."

Alexandra leaned forward and clasped her heels with her two hands and pulled herself forward until her chest rested on the floor. There was no denying that she was extremely flexible, as she moved through each of the poses to the maximum extent possible with little noticeable strain.

As I mimicked her movement, I tried not to glance between the legs of the yoga partners in front of me. I wished the young girl who'd I'd made a connection with had been positioned in front of me instead of to my side. As I leaned forward, I turned my head and glanced in her direction. She did the same, and we moved our chests forward and down in a synchronized manner. If yoga was all about the union of mind and body, I definitely was feeling yoked with my fantasy yoga partner.

"Press your pelvis into the floor," Alexandra said. "Bring your chest down and forward as far as you can. Spread your thighs apart with your hands as you feel the tension between your legs relax."

I glanced around the room and watched all the toned men and women bending over spreading their legs. My pussy grew wetter and wetter until I could hear the squishing of my legs against the mat as I rubbed my clit back and forth in the small puddle beneath me. I glanced over at the girl next to me and she smiled knowingly, as my pace of breathing increased and my eyes began to glaze over. I could have sworn her hips were rocking back and forth in lockstep with mine as we fantasized about rubbing our pussies together.

Please, I pleaded with her under my breath. *Please come back to the next session.*

Just when I was getting close to having a mini-orgasm, Alexandra asked us to sit up and change position.

Damn, girl, I thought. *You're such a tease.*

I was more convinced than ever that these poses were orchestrated to maximize the arc of our arousal just enough to deny us ultimate pleasure, so we'd have no choice but to come back and finish the deal.

"You're all doing fabulous," she purred in her soft, gentle intonation. "Now I want you to sit up with a straight back with your legs still spread out in front of you."

My eyes widened as she grabbed her big toes and began to lift them off the floor until they were at the same height as her head. She had opened herself up completely to the room, exposing her bare pussy and breasts in the most revealing way, daring us to ravish her magnificent body with our eyes.

"This is one of our most liberating poses," she said as she held her feet in the air, "where you'll feel most at one with your bodies and with those of your fellow yogis."

She glanced toward the back of the room at the two men and looked down between their legs.

"Don't worry if you notice some of your partners in a state of obvious arousal. This is a normal and healthy response and is just another way for us to connect with our bodies and feel the energy flowing through us. Try to keep your back straight and look up toward the ceiling as you lift your chest and breathe deeply. Feel your connection to the universe and the power within your own bodies. Free your mind and let all the negative chi flow from your body."

As I spread my legs and prepared to move into the provocative position, I rotated my hips slightly so I'd be facing closer to the girl next to me. I didn't want to make it too obvious what I was doing, but I was hoping she'd do the same so that we could look at one another's fully exposed bodies and I could let my fantasies run free. I began to lift my legs at a forty-five-degree angle to her and noticed out the corner of my eye that she had shifted her body subtly toward mine in a similar manner.

"Try to flex your PC muscle as you feel your Mula Bandha tighten and relax," Alexandra said. "This will create a stronger connection during intimate moments with your partner and heighten your sexual pleasure."

As I extended my legs and revealed my glistening pussy for the entire room to see, I looked over at the girl and smiled triumphantly. We'd opened ourselves up to one another in every sense of the word and let all of our inhibitions fall away while reveling in the beauty of one another's bodies. She was still turned just far enough away that I couldn't see her bare pussy behind her outstretched leg, but I noticed the puddle on the mat just in front of her.

She was just as turned on as I was!

My pussy quivered and shook in the excitement of the moment. If anyone had touched me anywhere near my Mula Bandha, I would have had an orgasm in a millisecond. My mind raced with all the possibilities I could engage in with my fantasy partner during the next level session. Just when I thought it couldn't get any more intense and intimate at that moment, Alexandra gave us a new instruction.

"Now," she said, "while still holding your toes as high in the air as you can, gently lean back with a straight back until you're balancing on your buttocks in a spread piked position."

She demonstrated the technique as she tipped slowly backwards then held a perfect forty-five degree piked position, looking up toward the ceiling in the sexiest but most composed manner.

God, I thought. *I'd fuck that woman any day—in any position.*

I glanced over at the girl behind me, and we both leaned backwards at the same time, matching the degree of rotation in perfect synchronicity. When we both reached the same forty-five-degree angle of our backs towards the floor, we beamed at one another in joy and pride at having achieved this level of proficiency. I wanted to turn my body completely in her direction and scoot my ass over to her then wrap my legs around her while we ground our pussies together and kissed passionately.

This naked yoga thing was even hotter than I'd hoped! I knew I'd be counting the minutes until the next session in horny anticipation.

I glanced in the mirror to see how this was working for the two men and saw that they had full hard-ons, angled straight up at forty-five degrees in the same direction as their outspread legs. What a turn-on this must have been for everybody in the room!

"I'm very proud of all of you," Alexandra said, as she began to lower her legs back toward the mat. "Now it's time for us to relax and return to a quiet state. Please bring your legs back onto your mats and cross them in front of you in the seated Buddha position. Close your eyes and reflect back on the growth you've achieved today. Breathe slowly in and out and feel the energy coursing through your body. You've all come a long way today. If you feel comfortable moving on to the next level, I hope to see you again where we'll explore a new level of synergy working together to stretch our minds and spirits even further."

Alexandra closed her eyes and placed the back of her hands on her knees as she touched her thumbs and forefingers together.

"Om," she chanted, exhaling slowly in an extended intonation.

"Om..." the room chanted with her in harmony, as our spirits exalted.

There was no question that I was ready to take this to the next level. I glanced out the corner of my eye at the girl next to me and winked as she returned my gaze.

I hope we'll see each other in a whole new light the next time we meet, I smiled to myself.

4

NAMASTE

On the evening of my second scheduled naked yoga session, I could hardly contain my excitement. This was the step up to Level 2, which Soraya had promised would involve closer interaction with the other yoga participants. I wasn't exactly sure what that meant, but I hoped it would involve some direct contact with a partner. I'd been fantasizing for the last three days about the girl who stretched beside me in the previous class, and my pussy was already tingling in anticipation of touching her.

When I arrived at the studio, I saw her stretching quietly on her mat. I immediately walked over to a spot in front of her and placed my mat on the floor to stake my claim. I didn't want anything getting in the way of direct access to her this time!

"Hi," I said, as she peered up at me. "I didn't properly introduce myself last time. My name's Jade."

"Kayla," she said, sitting up and extending her hand.

I leaned forward and shook her hand softly. Just touching her at the ends of our extremities was electrifying, but I pulled back when I felt my hand begin to moisten. Whether it was nerves or my body starting to heat up, it was undeniable that Kayla was getting me charged up just being next to her.

I sat down on my mat and crossed my legs in a comfortable seated position.

"I've been looking forward to this for *days*," I said. "That last class was pretty stimulating, don't you think?"

"Definitely," she said. "It's been running through my head on a continuous loop pretty much the whole time."

"So much for yoga calming our minds," I joked.

Kayla smiled.

"At least it accomplished the other goal of lifting our spirits and charging our bodies up."

"Yes, it certainly did."

I studied Kayla's face as she spoke to me, and I felt myself getting more and more attracted to her with each passing moment. She had a soft and gentle beauty that matched her petite figure. With bright green eyes and tiny freckles scattered over the bridge of her narrow nose, she looked like the consummate redhead that I'd often fantasized about. She'd be my first if we got that far, and I had no intention of letting her slip through my grasp.

At the top of the hour, a new instructor walked to the front of the room and laid her mat in front of the mirror. I wondered again if it might be Soraya from my initial online chat. She'd said there were only three tantric yoga instructors, so I figured there was a good chance I'd encounter her at one of the three stages.

"Good evening everyone," the instructor said. "My name's Amber and I'll be leading you through today's Level Two tantric session —Namaste."

"Namaste," some of the experienced yogis in the room repeated.

Amber placed her hands together in front of her chest and bowed gently.

"Namaste," she said, repeating the refrain. "How many of you know what this word means?"

I vaguely recalled Soraya talking about this in our online chat, but all I could remember was that it had something to do about showing respect for one another.

"Namaste comes from ancient Sanskrit meaning 'bowing to you,'"

Amber said. "In the context of yoga, it refers to the act of recognizing and bowing to the divinity within each of us. This will be the focus of today's session, where we partner up and celebrate the power within each of us as we seek to expand our limits. Accordingly, let's begin today's session by shedding our clothes and sharing the natural beauty within us."

Just as Alexandra had done in the previous session, Amber removed her tights and placed them in a neat pile by the mirror. She had a fuller, more athletic figure than Alexandra, but just as magnificent. Her full C-cup breasts bounced gently on her chest as she moved, and I was captivated by her large brown nipples. Her hips were wider than Alexandra's and she had curvier, more powerful-looking legs. The whole package projected a stunning hourglass figure. My eyes traced a line down to her narrow midsection, where a thin patch of brown pubic hair echoed the imagery of sand flowing through her body.

As I admired her beauty, I removed my own clothes, not wanting to be the last one with everyone staring at me again. When everyone was naked, Amber placed her hands in front of her chest once again and bowed to the group.

"Namaste," she said softly.

"Namaste," everyone in the group replied, bowing to her divinity.

I scanned the room in the mirror behind Amber and saw a few familiar faces, together with a number of new participants. This time the ratio of women to men wasn't quite as skewed, with roughly a dozen women and five or six men.

"Let's begin by getting comfortable with one another," Amber said. "I'd like you to turn to your nearest partner and stand facing him or her with your hands at your side. Straighten your back and elevate your chests as you breathe slowly in and out. You should see your partner's stomach extending and collapsing as they breathe from their diaphragms."

I turned toward Kayla before anyone else could steal her, and she did the same as she faced me. We smiled at one another knowing this time we'd be entirely focused on one another.

"Now, inhale as you raise your arms straight up and join your palms over your head," Amber instructed. "Feel the power within you as you stand tall as a mountain. Feel yourself rooted firmly to the ground as you tighten your thigh and buttock muscles. You are strong and magnificent, and you possess the power to achieve everything you desire. Look at your partner and recognize the strength within them."

Kayla and I looked at each other and smiled broadly. My grin kept widening until I showed my teeth, looking like I was posing for a camera shot. Kayla responded in kind, revealing the cutest dimples in the sides of her cheeks. This time, we didn't run our eyes over one another's bodies—we simply locked eyes and radiated the joy we were both feeling.

"Now take a large step forward with your right leg," Amber said. "Keep your hands above your head and squat down into a wide stance with your feet at least three or four feet apart. Hold this Warrior pose as you channel your chi and recognize how strong you are."

Kayla and I both took a broad step forward until our front foots were resting near the front of our mats. We'd suddenly closed half the distance between us, with only four or five feet separating us. My tummy sucked in an out as I gulped air to feed my straining legs. I couldn't keep my eyes from darting down between Kayla's scissored legs as I thought about touching her there. I noticed her breathing escalating too, and I wondered if it was due to the strain of holding the deep bend or from her own heightened arousal.

"Now," Amber continued, "with your feet, knees, and arms in the same locked position, rotate your upper body toward your left side until your chest is parallel with the line of your outstretched legs. Lower your arms and extend them straight across the same plane, holding them parallel to the floor. This is called the Warrior Two pose. Imagine you're lunging toward your partner in a fixed position, as if fencing with a foil. Except in this case, we're simply trying to touch fingers to channel the positive energy flowing between you."

Amber demonstrated the pose at the front of the room and we all followed her lead. There was now only a foot or so separating my outstretched hand from Kayla's. I shifted my weight forward onto my front leg to try to get closer.

"Keep your upper body centered between your front and rear foot," Amber said, "as you feel yourself grounded to the floor beneath you."

I frowned sheepishly at Kayla as I reluctantly pulled myself back and centered my weight as Amber instructed. Kayla giggled softly, recognizing my frustration. Our hips were turned away from each other so we could no longer see each other's bare midsections, but I had a commanding view of her tight ass, and I shamelessly took it all in.

"Now, place your left hand on the outside of your trailing leg and lift your right arm straight over your head, bending as far backwards with your chest still facing the side as you feel comfortable. You should feel your abs and intercostal muscles stretch as you expand and elevate your ribcage. This is called the Reverse Warrior pose."

Amber once again demonstrated the technique as she arched her body into position. She looked like the epitome of a yoga master as she struck the pose. With her legs spread wide and glancing up toward the ceiling with a focused expression, she looked for all the world like a true warrior.

Kayla and I shifted our weight, and dutifully adjusted our position. Unfortunately, we were now looking away from each other, and I was beginning to feel frustrated with the loss of connection. After a few people grunted from the tension of holding the pose, Amber instructed us to return to a seated position on our mats.

"Are you ready to begin working with your partners now to see if we can push one another to new heights?" she asked.

A few people nodded, and the rest of the room exhaled deeply, signaling they needed a brief respite.

"Let's return to the Buddha position to catch our breath for a moment," Amber said. "Cross your legs in front of you with your feet under your knees and hold your back straight while you breathe deeply to reenergize your muscles. Feel the tension leaving your body as you relax and free your mind. Close your eyes and feel the stillness of the room as you sense your pulse slowing and your thoughts emptying."

I closed my eyes, but it was impossible for me to empty my thoughts knowing I had a beautiful naked woman in front of me with whom I hoped to engage in closer contact.

"Okay," Amber said, breaking the silence after a few minutes of self-meditation. "We're now going to begin engaging in a more progressive manner with our fellow participants to see if we can push past some of our limits. I'd like you to move next to your partner and place your backs against one another, while you remain in the Buddha pose. This is called the Seated Meditation Bond. This will give you an opportunity to begin feeling your partner's energy in a safe and relaxing manner."

Kayla and I hesitated trying to figure out who should move first toward the other's mat, and I made the first move. I scooted over to her mat and gave her a soft kiss on her forehead before turning around and placing my back against hers. We assumed the cross-legged Buddha pose, and straightened our spines against one another, playfully pushing each other forward and back a few inches as we felt our bare skin and asses touching.

Amber noticed one of the participants was without a partner and walked over to one of the men. She clasped her hands in front of her and bowed, then sat down on his mat in the reverse meditation pose.

"Straighten your spines and feel your shoulder blades supporting one another," she said from her new position in the middle of the room. "Breathe deeply together as you feel each other's energy connecting your spines. Rest your hands on your knees as you channel your thoughts. Don't think about the fact that you're touching another stranger—simply be one."

I could feel Kayla's breathing as her upper back expanded and contracted, and she rested her head against my shoulder. I did the same, shifting my head to the other side, and we paused listening to each other's breathing. I wanted to reach around and touch her hand or her thigh, or touch my own dripping pussy, which had begun to dribble in excitement onto Kayla's mat. It took every ounce of my power to keep my hands where Amber instructed and just focus on relaxing.

Amber must have sensed that many of us were ready to move to the next stage when she asked us to reach around and touch our partners.

"Now, with your backs still pressed together, twist your upper bodies gently to your left and place your left hand on the outside of your right knee. With your right arm, reach around your partner's back and place it on the inside of his or her thigh. This is a trust-building exercise that permits you to help each other stretch, while also beginning to feel more comfortable with one another."

Kayla and I looked toward Amber to follow the correct technique, as we watched her reach around her partner's back and wedge her straight arm against the inside of his opposite thigh. It was impossible from our position to witness the man's reaction, but I was certain it would be getting a rise out of him.

We twisted our bodies as Amber indicated, and I could feel my arm shaking as I reached behind Kayla's back and placed my hand on her inner thigh. When she did the same, my back shook from the sexual energy that shot through me. By now, my inner thighs were coated with the slippery juices streaming out of my pussy, and Kayla squeezed her fingers against my leg to avoid slipping off. I couldn't feel any wetness on the inside of her thigh—just the soft, exquisite warmth of her smooth skin. I was glad that I'd shaved my legs the previous day, hoping she'd revel in my soft skin as much as I was hers.

Amber interrupted our thoughts with another command.

"Gently press down and outward with your two hands as you feel you and your partner move your knees closer to the floor. Focus on the pressure and nonverbal feedback from your partner to know how far you can push without causing pain or discomfort. Listen to your partner's body and trust one another to help stretch and relax."

As I pushed gently down on Kayla's thigh and felt her do the same, I felt my adductor muscle begin to relax as our knees moved closer to the floor. I was careful to go slow, paying close attention to the tension in Kayla's leg so I never pushed her beyond her limits. Within a minute or so, both of our legs were pressed flat against the floor. I could still feel some tension in my inner thighs, but much more in my aching pussy from the proximity of her hand to my slit. I hoped that Amber's next instruction would bring us even closer together, where we might actually be able to touch our private parts.

"Now let's turn around facing each other while we twist in the other direction," she instructed. I want you to face each other, returning to the cross-legged Buddha position, with your knees touching one another. Reach as far around your back with your right hand while you extend your other hand forward and clasp your partner's hand behind their back. Gently hold and pull one another as you twist your upper bodies away from one another."

Once again, we watched Amber as she demonstrated the technique with her partner, then we followed suit. I was pleased with how the progression of moves were now being staged in a manner that our level of engagement with our partners increased each time. Kayla and I playfully pushed and pulled each other as we rocked our upper bodies from side to side. It was a fun, stress-free way for us to wind down from the excitement of our last pose, but I was looking forward to rocking our bodies in a whole other way.

"Okay," Amber said. "Now let's see if we can help each other stretch our lower half."

Yes! I screamed inside. *My lower half needs some serious attention.*

Finally, I'd get a chance to touch Kayla where I'd fantasized for so many hours. Our heads turned to look at one another and our eyes widened as we processed the same thought. I could see Kayla's pupils dilating with rising excitement.

"First," Amber instructed, "get into the staff position facing each other with your legs extended straight out in front of you. Touch each other's feet and place your palms face down on the floor beside your hips. Then lean forward with outstretched arms and try to grasp each other's hands. If you can, gently pull one partner toward the other while he or she bends forward with a straight back.

"As always, feel the tension in your partner's body and listen to their feedback so you can help them stretch their muscles without any discomfort. Your goal is to help your partner reach beyond their self-imposed limits, in a safe and supportive role. If you can't reach far enough forward to touch your partner's hands, then simply place your hands on your own legs and try to inch toward him or her with the goal of touching."

This was an easy one for Kayla and me, since we both had excellent flexibility. I was able to guide her all the way forward until her face touched her legs just below her knee, then she repeated the sequence for me. I loved the idea of her head moving closer to my box and it was tempting to separate my legs a little bit to give her a view of my pussy. We were so close together now that our arms bent awkwardly, so we moved our hands further up each other's arms to make it easier to hold each another in the flexed position.

After two or three minutes, Amber asked us to focus on our opposite partner, as she allowed the man to pull her forward, holding her hands. Kayla and I giggled at how we'd gotten ahead of Amber's instruction and simply repeated our steps. After another three or four minutes, Amber asked us to return to the staff position and place our hands in our laps.

"I hope you enjoyed that and found you were able to push yourself a little further than you normally could on your own. Now we're going to stretch another important muscle in our lower legs, which is the adductor muscle between our thighs. I want you to keep your legs extended, but now spread them as far apart as you can. Then move yourself forward until you're touching your partner's feet once again and lean forward to join hands. It should be easier for you to reach your partner this time, as your hips will be closer together. As before, gently pull one partner at a time toward the other while he or she leans forward with a straight back, trying to move your upper body as close to the floor as possible. Breathe deeply, and only go as far as you feel comfortable."

I wasn't sure if the 'feeling comfortable' part Amber referred to concerned the tension we were about to feel in our adductor muscles, or the unease some people might have getting so close to one another's private parts. But I was feeling no such compunction, I wanted to get as close to Kayla's private parts as I could, as soon as possible!

Sensing each other's rising excitement, Kayla and I immediately spread our legs and reached out our arms to one another. I was dying to look at her exposed pussy, but I knew that I'd have a better chance to do so soon. We both hesitated, unsure as to who should 'go down' first, and I gently pulled her toward me to break our little tug of war.

"Feel the pressure in the muscles between your legs," Amber called out. "Only go far enough to where it begins to bind, then pause and breathe slowly until you feel the muscles relax. Listen to your partner's body as you guide them lower and further."

Amber had little trouble bending all the way forward, until once again her upper body was resting flat on the floor between her outstretched legs.

"If you're able to go all the way down," Amber said, "spread your legs further apart and repeat the process, inching closer and closer to your partner. Pay no mind if you notice your partner is getting aroused, as this is a normal and healthy response in this situation. Focus on a spot on the floor in front of you if it makes you feel more comfortable, as you listen to your own body and feel yourself relax and elongate."

Kayla and I pressed our feet together and pushed our legs further apart. Our legs were now at a sixty-degree angle facing one another and there was no escaping the fact that our open pussies were facing one another. I pulled Kayla gently toward me once again, clasping her arms closer to her elbow as she leaned her head down, closer to my quivering love box. I wasn't sure if she was looking at me there as she bent over, but if she was, she must have noticed the widening puddle that was forming between my legs. My labia quivered, and I could feel my hood retract as my excited clitoris pushed out into the open. She couldn't have missed how turned on I was, the closer her head got to my pussy.

Amber's gentle voice continued to encourage us in the background.

"You can focus on taking your partner as far as he or she feels comfortable going in one continuous stretch, or alternate back and forth as each of you extend your position forward."

I glanced in Amber's direction and saw her bent closer toward her partner as he pulled her arms toward him. I could have sworn I saw the head of his erect penis sticking up between his legs as she moved her naked body in his direction. But her flexibility was so pronounced that with her legs spread almost fully apart, her head was closer to his chest than his groin as she bent forward. Perhaps this was by design, as I'm sure it must have been awkward for her to get so intimate with an apparent stranger in this group setting.

I was hoping that Kayla wanted to continue stretching in my direction, until either her head or her pussy touched mine. By now, my clit was throbbing in excitement, and I was gushing lubrication all over the mat. Any kind of direct contact would have pushed me over the edge in an instant, and I was desperately seeking release.

Maybe Kayla was feeling the same way or maybe she was feeling a bit shy, because just as her face got to within a few inches of my steaming pussy, she leaned back and smiled.

"Your turn," she purred.

She started to pull me toward her as we pushed our feet even wider apart. Our legs were now more than ninety degrees sepa-rated and our pussies were only a foot or so apart. As Amber had with her partner, we'd spread our legs so wide and were so close together, that when I leaned forward, my head touched her chest instead of her pussy. I was just about to kiss one of her erect nipples and suck her into my mouth when Amber interrupted us again.

"If your feet are wide enough apart that you can no longer lean all the way forward, try having your partner lean back in order to guide you further forward and down. The goal is to stretch and elongate your adductor muscles without actually touching any other part of your bodies. If you can widen your feet still further, your other goal is to bring your Mula Bandha locks as close together as possible without actually touching. We'll save that for your last level of tantric training."

No touching? I thought. *Screw that! If somebody doesn't touch my Mula Bandha soon, I'm going to explode.*

Kayla sensed my desperation and pulled my face toward her chest until my lips touched her skin. She wasn't going to have any part of this no-touching rule either. But instead of allowing me to linger and savor her sweet breasts and nipples, she began to lean back as Amber instructed, pulling me forward and my head lower down her abdomen. But because we'd spread our legs so far apart, we'd gotten too close to bring our heads any closer to our pussies than each other's belly buttons.

Kayla wrapped her arms around my waist and pulled me closer toward her as our legs spread even wider apart. Our pussies were now less than six inches apart with our legs spread in a near one-hundred-and-eighty-degree angle facing one another, and I swore I could feel the heat emanating from her hole as we strained to touch one another. How I wanted to feel her tender clit touch mine and join our love juices together. There was something far more intimate and sexy about this kind of touching than the rough and tumble tribbing I'd experienced in the dark room with my last lesbian lover.

"Remember," Amber intoned from the center of the room, "you should only be touching each other with your hands and feet. Part of the fun is feeling the energy transferring between the two of you as you get closer and closer to reaching your limits. Push your hips forward but respect your partner's space. Get as close to one another as you can without touching and feel the energy passing between you."

I glanced over at Amber and saw that she and the man had reached the point where their chests and hips almost touched, but they had their eyes closed with barely an inch separating them. I felt sorry for her partner, imagining his blue balls and his cock twitching in anticipation with her pussy so close.

Screw that idea, I thought.

Kayla and I both wrapped our arms around one another's waist and we pulled each other firmly toward each other as our sweaty chests rubbed together. I could feel the warm puddle between us on the mat as our thighs connected further up toward our pussies, and we both shifted our hips trying to touch ourselves. When we finally did, the feeling was electrifying. We held each other close and kissed passionately, stifling our moans as we came in each other's mouths. Kayla swirled her tongue in my mouth as she ground her hips against mine, and our chests heaved against one another in simultaneous orgasms.

At that moment, I didn't care who was watching or how many rules we were breaking. Kayla and I had reached a true union of souls and found our own place of enlightenment.

5

HARMONY

When the day of my scheduled third session of tantric yoga came around, my entire body was buzzing with excitement. The last session had exceeded my expectations, and I felt I'd formed an amazing bond with Kayla. The connection we'd made was tender, deep, and thrilling. I couldn't wait to touch her again and feel her soft skin against mine. Soraya had said the third level would be where we truly joined our minds, bodies, and spirits and where we'd be able to explore our partner's bodies more intimately. Even though Kayla and I had already broken the rule about no intimate touching at the last session, I felt there was much further we could go.

I arrived at the yoga studio fifteen minutes early so I'd have a chance to chat with Kayla before we began the routines. She hadn't arrived yet, so I walked to the back of the room and placed my mat in a spot near the window. I wanted to have a little more privacy this time, where we'd be more sheltered from the prying eyes of the rest of the group. As more and more people filtered into the room, I watched the clock on the wall move closer to our appointed start time. There was still no sign of Kayla, and I started to worry. We'd promised to meet again for this session, but I'd felt it was too early to ask for her number. Was she having second thoughts? Was she feeling too embarrassed to come back after our intimate exposure at the last session?

The room was beginning to fill and by now there were only a few spots remaining on the floor upon which to lay a mat. An attractive woman in her late-20s paused at an open patch next to me.

"Is this spot taken?" she asked, in a sexy voice.

"Um—no..." I hesitated, looking up at the clock.

"Thank you," she said, smiling at me warmly. She laid her mat about three feet away from me and placed her belongings next to it on the floor. She had long dark hair pulled back in a bun and was wearing loose-fitting sweats and a T-shirt. I could see the outline of her figure in her clothes, and her firm breasts thrust out prominently in her loose shirt. She had an exotic beauty, maybe East-European I thought, with sharp cheekbones and an angular jaw. There was something mysterious and sexy about her that I found uniquely attractive.

"I'm Neve," she said, reaching out her hand.

"Jade," I said, stealing a final glance at the clock as I shook her hand.

At 7:00 p.m., a new instructor entered the room and closed the door behind her. I felt a knot in my stomach knowing that Kayla wasn't coming, and I began to worry if something had happened to her. I was already regretting not getting her number.

The instructor strode to the front of the room and smiled at some of the people she recognized. She had medium length blond hair tied back in a braided pony tail and a petite figure. She was much slimmer than Alexandra or Amber, maybe only five feet three inches tall and barely a hundred pounds. But I could see the sinewy muscles flexing in her tight yoga outfit as she moved. She was pretty in a girl-next-door kind of way, with large brown eyes and fair skin. Could this be the mysterious Soraya that I'd talked to in the online chat session?

"Good evening, everybody," she said, addressing the group. "Welcome to our Level Three Tantric Yoga session—Harmony. My name's Soraya, and I'll be leading this evening's session. I hope you found your last session stimulating. Tonight, we're going to step it up with some new exercises and with a greater level of engagement with your partners. This final level is where we seek maximum enlightenment through the union of our minds, bodies, and spirits. Are we ready to get started?"

Everybody in the room nodded enthusiastically, except me. Even though the 'union of bodies' was what I had signed up for, part of me felt lost without Kayla at my side. It was hard to imagine how I'd be able to engage so intimately with anyone else right now.

"Okay then," Soraya said. "Let's begin by celebrating the freedom of our natural selves by removing our clothes."

By now, everyone had become comfortable with the notion of stretching in the buff, and it didn't long for the group to get naked. I scanned the room through the expanse of mirrors on the front wall and saw many familiar faces. Most of the people from my last class had returned, together with a few new faces who were stepping up from another Level Two class. Once again, the women outnumbered the men by a ratio of two to one, but I noticed that some of the men had paired up next to one another this time. I'd sensed that some of the men attending our previous sessions were gay, and I was intrigued to see how they'd engage one another in this advanced session.

I quickly checked out Soraya's body as my eyes darted across her naked figure. She had a perfect ballerina's figure, with strong slender muscles, small but shapely breasts, and narrow hips with a round, firm ass. She smiled as she appraised the diverse group standing naked before her.

"First," she began, "let's recognize the power within each of us by turning to our partner and celebrating their beauty. Turn to face your nearest colleague and stand with your feet together, with your spine erect. Feel the strength in their body and celebrate the unique beauty each of us embodies."

Up to this point, I'd only seen the backside of Neve as we both faced the front of the room with her slightly in front of me. I'd admired her strong and shapely ass and was looking forward to seeing what she looked like from the front. But as she turned around to face me, my mouth dropped open. A strange movement between her legs drew my gaze down to her midsection, where she had a prominent hanging penis.

My eyes flew open as I caught my breath, and she smiled at me with a knowing gaze. Far from being scared or offended by her transgender appearance, I was fascinated by her blend of masculine and feminine traits. Other than the large phallus hanging between her legs, no one would have guessed that she was transgender. Her arms and legs were slender like a woman's, and her waist tapered in the middle to accent the roundness of her hips. She had a flat and nicely toned stomach that blended seamlessly with her large, firm breasts. I knew that they were likely fake, but I didn't care—they were perfectly shaped, firm, and round. I couldn't see any visible sign of scarring, and her nipples were large and protruded proudly, as if telling me: 'I'm a woman!'

I couldn't help my eyes from darting over her voluptuous figure, but I lingered especially long at her magnificent tool. It was long and thick even in a flaccid state, perfectly circumcised, and a lovely shade of light brown, matching the rest of her beautifully tanned body. She'd shaved her pubic patch to a barely visible light brown stubble, and her tight balls were clean and bare. I could feel my breathing increasing in excitement as my chest rose and fell from the thrill of seeing my first transgender person naked.

Was she a man, a woman, a transsexual, or a lady-boy? I wondered. *What was the correct term to call transgender people these days?*

From the feminine pitch of her voice, I knew she was a man who was probably taking hormone treatment to become a woman, and for all intents and purposes, that's what she looked and sounded like to me. All except that glorious joystick hanging between her legs. My pussy unconsciously began to lubricate thinking of all the fun I could have with her. Suddenly, the image of Kayla was far from my mind.

I looked up at Neve and smiled. The only judging she'd receive from me today was positive affirmation and admiration. I lifted my chest and thrust out my breasts, silently signaling: 'Look at us—two beautiful, strong, proud, women.' She beamed back at me and pulled her feet apart a couple of inches. I glanced down at her member and noticed that it had swelled in size since I last looked at it. Still pointing downwards, it had lengthened to at least six inches in length and five inches in girth.

If this is what her cock looks like when it's tame, I can't wait to see what it looks like fully excited.

The sound of Soraya's voice pulled me out of my trance.

"Now let's loosen up a little bit in preparation for some new poses," she said. "Extend your arms straight over your head and clasp your hands together. Now bend slightly to your right side, keeping your chest parallel with the rest of your body. Bend as far as you can, then pause and hold while you breathe from your diaphragm."

Neve and I swung our bodies in opposite directions as we looked at each other, tilting our heads playfully. After a minute or so, Soraya asked us to bend to the opposite side, and our smiles broadened as Neve and I continued tilting our heads like schoolgirls.

"Now, stand up straight in the Mountain pose, then step back about one leg length with your left foot as you bend your right knee to a ninety-degree angle. This variation on the Warrior pose will strengthen your thighs and glutes, and channel the power within you. Hold for one minute, then switch and repeat with the opposite side."

Neve and I extended our legs and sunk down into the pose, as we looked at each other with exaggerated looks of ferocity on our faces. When we switched to the other side, our eyes widened and our lips puckered, while we continued play-acting. It was nice to have someone to partner with who didn't take the whole naked yoga thing too seriously. Her pecker detumesced slightly, and it swung gently between her legs whenever we changed positions. I could tell she was getting more relaxed and focusing on enjoying the moment.

"Now bend your upper body forward," Soraya instructed, "and place your hands on the floor beside your front foot. You should feel the stretch in your right hamstring and left thigh. Lower yourself as far as you can and hold the position as you look up, breathing slowly."

Neve and I faced each other directly and we continued our little game, holding our warrior expressions as our faces came closer together. I glanced up and down her body to signal I was checking out the firehose between her legs, and with each glance it seemed to get bigger and bigger. It was fun to have so much control over a cock, even if it didn't belong to a man.

"Ok," Soraya continued. "Now let's work on our balance for a little bit before we get into some more serious poses. Turn away from your partners and return to the standing forward fold. Bend over and place your fingertips on the floor then sweep your right leg up to a ninety-degree angle behind you. Now turn your chest to the left and reach up with your left arm until it's pointing toward the ceiling. Hold and pause, trying to center your body over your left leg."

Neve and I watched Soraya demonstrate the technique, then we mimicked her position. We couldn't see each other faced in opposite directions, so I lowered my head and glanced between my legs. She waved her foot that was pointed in my direction as if to say hello and giggled softly. I could see her testicles nestled tightly between her extended legs and her cock pointing straight down. I wondered if she noticed the shining wet spot that was forming between my own legs. Soraya asked us to repeat the procedure on the other side, and once again Neve and I stole glances at each other's backsides between our scissored legs.

"Now we're going to try something a little more risqué," she said. "It's called the Standing Split. Return to the standing forward fold position, continuing in the opposite directions to your partner. Brace your fingertips against the floor and sweep your right leg straight up toward the ceiling. Keep your hips squared and inhale, extending your chest. Now, exhale and lean toward your standing leg, bracing your left forearm against your left calf. Lift your right leg as high and straight as you can, feeling the stretch in your glutes and hamstrings."

As I bent over into the revealing position, I smiled knowing that Soraya could just as easily instructed us to perform the pose facing our partners. But this way, we were completely opening ourselves up to one another, revealing our most intimate parts only inches away from one another.

I was able to lift my foot high enough that my legs were in an almost straight line, with my chest resting against my left thigh. I opened my eyes and looked over at Neve and saw that she was straining to hold the position but had managed to get her legs into a near one-hundred-and-fifty-degree angle. I nodded in approval as she smiled at me, breathing heavily. Her balls had pulled slightly toward her cock from the force of gravity, and I could see her exposed perineum and anus between her upswept leg. I admired how clean and bare everything was, and I hoped she was inspecting me as closely as I was her. I could feel a trickle of lubrication leaking out of my pussy and beginning to run down my leg as I noticed her penis swell and elongate. It was exhilarating to communicate exactly what we were feeling purely through our body language.

After a couple of minutes, Soraya asked us to switch positions and stretch the other leg. I could feel the slick liquid between my thighs as they scissored together. A few people in the group groaned trying to hold the pose, and Soraya asked us to return to a comfortable standing position.

"Okay," she said. "You can turn around and face your partners again. Let's rest for a moment before we try some seated poses. I want you to sit down on your mat and cross your legs in the Buddha position, then place your palms on your knees and close your eyes. Breathe deeply, relaxing your muscles. Empty your thoughts as you feel the energy emanating from within you and from your partner.

"Om," Soraya hummed out loud.

"Om," everyone in the group chanted in return.

"Now let's limber up our back and work on strengthening our core," she said. "Extend your legs straight in front of you, then lift your right knee, placing your right foot against the inside of your left thigh. Now, twist gently to your right and bring your left arm to rest on the outside of your elevated knee. Brace your upper body by placing your right hand behind you on the floor as you try to twist your torso as far as you can in the opposite direction."

I remembered this move from our last class and wondered what Soraya's plan was for this session's development. Maybe it was simply designed to let us come down from the intensity of the last exercise, but I was definitely ready to step it up to the next level of engagement. Neve and I tried not to look at one another as we turned our heads to guide our chests in opposite directions. But when we switched to focus on the other side, we stole a quick glance and smiled at each other.

Maybe there was method to Soraya's madness after all, I thought. The brief pause in the sexual tension that had been building up between us only seemed to heighten my desire.

"Okay," Soraya said, "now let's get down to the serious stuff. Bring your legs back in front of you and extend them straight out until they're touching your partner's feet. Now gently spread your legs as far apart as you can, feeling the stretch in your inner thigh muscles. Extend your arms toward your partner and clasp each other's hands as you brace your feet together. Have one partner gently pull the other forward, bringing your chest as far forward and low as you can. Breathe slowly and deeply, pausing when it starts to bind. When you feel your muscles relax, spread your feet a little further apart and try to bend even lower."

I remembered this pose vividly from our last class. This had been the one that brought Kayla and me close enough where we came together. I wondered if Soraya had a different design for us this time. If this session was all about creating a closer union between partners, I was ready for whatever she had in mind. Neve and I placed our feet together and gradually spread our legs apart as we stared into each other's eyes. Neither of us wanted to be the first to leer openly at the other's exposed genitalia.

When our legs were spread as far as they could go, we hesitated holding hands, wondering who should 'go first'. As with Kayla, I decided to take the lead. I gently pulled Neve towards me, and she lowered her chest and head between my legs. As her head got closer to my throbbing pussy, I wondered what it would be like to make love with a transsexual. I'd never had a transgendered person go down on me, and my clit tingled with the thought of Neve wrapping her lips around my love button.

She wasn't quite as flexible as Kayla, but with her legs swung out over ninety degrees, she was able to get her face very close to my sopping pussy. I held her arms firmly, holding her in the extended position to give her a moment to revel in my womanness. I wasn't sure what her sexual preferences were, but I knew she identified as a woman and I wanted her to see my female parts in all their glory, close-up. I heard her exhale in a muffled moan as she lingered, taking it all in. I was tempted to spread my legs further to see if she could get close enough to touch me, when I heard Soraya's voice again.

"After one partner has stretched as far as he or she can go, switch positions and guide the other to do the same. You may notice your partner's arousal, and this is perfectly normal. If it helps to provide extra motivation for your partner, you may wish to touch each other in the Mula Bandha area to encourage them to go further. Of course, we always want to respect our partner's personal space, so if you want to disengage at any time, just provide the signal."

I released the tension on Neve's arms and she lifted her torso up, looking at me quizzically. I suspect she had the same idea as me and had hoped to go further. I smiled at her and looked down between her legs. Her cock was fully erect and pointing up toward her belly. Now at least eight inches in length, it had to be six inches around. It was perfectly straight and glistening at the tip. I had a feeling she needed to be touched even more than I did.

She nodded to indicate that she understood my plan and gently began to pull my arms toward her. I knew that I'd have no difficulty getting all the way down to her crotch, so I teased her by lowering myself slowly. I could see her erect cock bouncing from the pulse coursing through it, and I licked my lips in anticipation of taking it into my mouth. The angle of our legs was perfectly positioned for my head to reach the top of her erection with my back straight. I paused with my lips inches away from her swelling and glistening head. I was dying to swallow her like a popsicle, but I wanted to build her sexual tension even more. I wanted to hear her gasp when I finally took her into my mouth.

I could see the pre-cum streaming out of her slit as she vainly thrust her hips up toward my face. I paused for one last moment, then placed my lips around the head of her dick and sucked her into my mouth. She let out a guttural moan as I felt her lingham swell in my mouth. I pictured her sitting on her yoga mat, sitting with her legs spread wide, with everyone watching me suck this beautiful woman's cock into my mouth. Maybe they were doing the same thing at this moment, because I could hear muffled moans coming from the people around me. Whether they were getting turned on watching us or getting some of their own action, it didn't matter. At this moment, I was at one with my partner.

As I swirled my tongue around the head of Neve's cock and pushed myself down deeper over her shaft, I heard the pace of her breathing increase. She started to whimper when I flicked the sensitive part of her coronal ridge under the head of her frenulum. I sensed that she was getting close to cumming, so I moved my hands from my sides and cradled her balls, rolling and squeezing them gently in my hands.

"Oh God," she gasped, as I felt her hard cock flex in my mouth.

It won't be long now, I thought.

Just then, I heard Soraya's voice again, as she instructed us to move into a new position.

You've got to be kidding me.

"I know many of you are feeling an intimate connection with your partners," she said. "If you wish to continue exploring this position, you may. But we have one last pose that I think you may find even more empowering. It's called the Buddha Straddle, and I believe you may find it brings you even closer together and elevates your spirits even higher. When you're ready, sit up and face your partner in the seated Buddha position."

I paused for a moment with Neve's throbbing cock in my mouth, and she froze, unsure what to do next. Then she gently placed her hands under my shoulders and encouraged me to lift myself up. I withdrew her cock from my mouth, kissed the tip, then sat up. The look we shared when our eyes met said everything we needed to express. Her eyes were glazed over and she gave me a thankful smile. Whether she was trying to respect Soraya's commands or she was trying to save herself for the main event, I wasn't sure. I simply smiled back at her as I gazed deeply into her eyes.

"Okay," Soraya said, after everyone had moved into the new position. "Place your hands together in front of your chest and bow toward your partner to acknowledge each other's divinity."

Neve and I pressed our hands together in a steepled prayer position and bowed.

"Namaste," Soraya said.

"Namaste," Neve and I said, saluting each other.

"In this last exercise," Soraya said, "we're going to move as close together as we possibly can to combine our life energy into one. I'd like one partner to move forward and lift yourself up so your hips rest between the straddled legs of your other partner. Then wrap your legs around your partner's hips and interlock your feet to pull yourself toward him or her. You may choose to simply rest in this position as you listen to each other meditate, or you may engage your Mula Banha directly in order to exchange your energy more intimately. Either way, focus on each other's breathing and move slowly to celebrate each other's life flow."

I smiled at Neve and scooted toward her, then lifted myself up into her lap. We both knew who should be on top in this case. I could feel her cock pressing against my stomach, and I paused as I looked into her eyes.

"Enjoy," I whispered softly.

Then I tilted my hips forward and grasped the shaft of her cock between my slick labia and rocked slowly back and forth to massage her gently. She closed her eyes to savor the sensation, and I moved forward to kiss her. Her lips were soft and pliant, and I pushed my tongue inside her, allowing her to taste her own honey. We kissed for a time with me rubbing her shaft up and down my slippery slit, then we both tilted our hips at the same time and her cock slipped inside me. We both moaned as we held each other close, then Neve titled her hips further as I sunk down onto her throbbing member. I was surprised I could take all of her inside me, and we began to rock our hips faster together.

"Remember to go slow," Soraya admonished. "One of the joys of tantric yoga is the savoring of each other's Chi as we interweave our bodies and join together in intimate connection. Enjoy the feeling and savor each moment, as you prolong the build-up of your pleasure and intimacy. Feel the power coursing through your bodies and the joy that you're able to share with one another."

Neve and I slowed our rocking down and I placed my head beside hers as we held each other close. I looked behind her for a moment and watched some of the other couples in the room. Some of them were engaged in girl-girl coupling and some were engaged in man-to-man intercourse. But most, like Neve and me, were engaged in heterosexual coupling. As I ground my hips against Neve's cock, I watched the other couples moving in a similar fashion. Many were looking into each other's eyes or were locked in a passionate kiss.

Grunts and moans were coming from around the room now, and I could hear the passion rising between each couple. Not far away, I could see two men rocking their hips together, as their joined cocks poked up from their laps, their tips shining in the bright light streaming in from the window. It was an incredible turn-on watching everybody connecting with their partners as they focused on being in the moment.

I could feel my juices starting to flow more freely now as they dribbled out of my hole and down Neve's balls onto our shared mat. I could feel her tight balls rubbing against my perineum and knew she was getting close. But I was determined not to be the first ones to come this time, and I slowed down our rhythm to give her a chance to ease off. I think she had the same idea, and she stopped rocking her hips to let me take over creating the friction. I could feel the warmth of her cock deep inside me as the heat radiated between us. I began kissing her again and we closed our eyes as we rolled our tongues inside each other's mouths.

"Feel the energy radiating between you," Soraya said from the front of the room. For a moment, I felt sorry that she hadn't been able to partner up with anyone else, since there was an even number of participants in this class and everyone was coupled up. I wondered if she might be playing with herself watching this incredibly erotic show. I could hear the breathing and moaning of my colleagues around me, and Neve and I began to increase our pace. We wouldn't be the first to come, but I didn't want to be the last, either.

As we heard some couples groan out loud in the obvious throes of orgasm, Neve suddenly began moving her hips again, thrusting her cock deeper inside me. I returned the favor and pressed my cunt as hard as I could against the base of her cock and balls. We were joined as deep and close as two people could be, and I could feel her breathing increasing in speed and intensity as she neared the precipice. With one final thrust, she pushed inside me as I clamped down on her penis and felt the throbbing of her cock as she emptied her potion inside me. That was enough to put me over the edge, and I pulled her hips toward me as I locked my legs around her. I arched my back and came in one long stream of continuing spasms for what seemed like a minute. My body shook as I savored every last second of the euphoria we shared.

When we finally came down from our powerful orgasms, we held each other close and touched our foreheads as we closed our eyes. There was utter silence in the room as everyone including Soraya concentrated on the fulfillment we all felt. I said a silent prayer as I thanked the universe for sharing its energy with me and Neve.

"Om," I purred into her ear.

"Om," she replied, as I felt her cock twitch one last time inside my pussy.

THE DINNER PARTY - PREVIEW

FINGER FOOD

S ometime later, I heard a soft tap on my bedroom door. Not wanting to remove myself just yet from my cocoon of luxury, I called out to answer.

"Yes?"

"It's time for your massage," a woman's voice replied.

"Just one minute please."

I reluctantly stepped out of the bath and quickly toweled myself dry. I wrapped a large bath sheet around me, re-donned my mask, then opened the bedroom door.

A petite young Asian girl greeted me, wearing a kimono similar to mine and a crimson masquerade mask.

Apparently not everybody who works here always walks around stark naked.

The girl was utterly breathtaking. Long jet-black hair cascaded over high cheekbones past pouty lips, her delicate collarbones peeking from the top of her kimono. I could see her breasts and hips outlined by the tightly-wrapped kimono and suddenly wished that she too had come to my boudoir naked.

"My name is Jasmine," she said. "I'm your personal masseuse and esthetician. Are you ready for your final preparation?

Just the thought of this beauty laying her tender hands on me sent a shiver down my spine.

"Definitely. Please come in. How would you like me to prepare?"

"Come with me, please."

Jasmine led me into the bathroom, where she nonchalantly removed her kimono and hung it behind the bathroom door.

Oh my God.

I didn't think anyone in this place could get more beautiful or sensuous. Jasmine had perfectly shaped B-cup breasts with a thin indentation running down the center of her perfectly toned stomach. Like everyone else in this place, her pubis was utterly bald and flawless. She barely looked eighteen and I was just about to ask her age, but she spoke first.

"If you'd like to remove your towel and lay face down on the table, we can get started. May I call you Jade?"

There was something about her confident manner and tone that belied her youthful appearance. I had no inhibitions whatsoever about displaying myself unclothed to this stranger.

"Yes, thank you, Jasmine." I unhooked my bath sheet and threw it against the side of the tub.

"Would you like me to drape your backside?" Jasmine asked.

"That won't be necessary," I quickly answered.

Jasmine walked over to the vanity counter and picked up two small bottles of oil resting under an orange radiant lamp. She brought them back to the massage table, opened one, and poured the oil into one cupped hand then rubbed her hands together. The scent of lavender wafted toward my nose.

I closed my eyes in anticipation of her touch. I'd had massages before, but nothing as sensuous and stimulating as this. When her hands touched the small of my back, I jerked reflexively from the sexual tension. My heart was beating a hundred miles an hour as I felt the blood coursing through my veins.

Jasmine must have sensed my nervous tension and began

pressing her fingers more firmly into my back as she moved them slowly up each side of my spine. The warm oil allowed her hands to glide effortlessly across my skin. She used every surface of her hands to massage my muscles, expertly kneading my skin with her fingers and palm.

I began to relax as my muscles softened and surrendered to her touch. She sensuously massaged every part of my back, shoulders, and neck, applying just the right amount of pressure. Periodically, she would pour more warm oil on my lower back, dipping her hands in it to replenish the silky lubrication against my pliant skin.

Just as the sexual tension began to subside from the utter relaxation of the massage, Jasmine moved her hands down to my buttocks and began to caress them in soft circular motions. My glutes contracted involuntarily and I unconsciously pressed my mound into the firm padding of the table. Suddenly I was quickly reminded that a gorgeous young woman was caressing my naked body. She cupped each buttock between her hands as she massaged my ass tantalizingly, her little finger sliding slowly into the cleft just above my anus.

Periodically, I'd partially open one of my eyes with my head turned in her direction to look at her gorgeous body. My head was at the same level as her midsection, and my mouth watered as I watched her stomach muscles flex and her hips undulate with each movement of her hands. At times her pussy was almost right beside me and I wanted to reach out and run my own fingers up her soft legs.

I was in total heaven and getting wetter by the moment. Just when I thought I couldn't stand it anymore, she suddenly moved her hands down to my feet and began massaging her thumbs into my soles.

I'd always loved having my feet massaged, but nobody did it like Jasmine. She cradled my foot and used every part of her hands to massage and knead every surface from my heel to my toes. I didn't want her to stop, but there were other parts of my body that were screaming for attention.

As if reading my thoughts, she began moving her hands up toward my calf, using her thumbs to spread the muscle apart. She lingered almost as long on my calf as she had on my foot, rolling the ball of my calf between both of her hands, sliding her slick hands up and down erotically. I couldn't help imagining how she might use those same hands to massage a man's erect cock in a similar manner. My mind wandered again to what pleasures lay in wait for me over dinner.

After shifting her hands to my right leg and giving my other foot and calf similar attention, she placed each hand just behind my knees and began to slowly move them up towards my buttocks. Her thumbs pressed against my inner thighs as she glided tantalizingly close to my apex.

I rolled my legs outward in an invitation to move closer. My legs were parted enough that I was sure she could see my vulva from her vantage point behind me. In my highly aroused state, my lips were engorged and spread apart, revealing my moist and quivering opening.

But as much as I desperately wanted her to, Jasmine never touched me there. She repeatedly slid her hands right up to the edge of my slit, pressing and rotating her thumbs on the fleshy meat of my upper thighs just below my aching pussy. I suppose this was part of her master plan—to tease me mercilessly and inflame my passions so I'd be ready for just about anything at the main event.

It was certainly working. After thirty minutes of Jasmine's ministrations, I was grinding my pussy into the table trying desperately to give my clit some needed direct stimulation.

Just when I thought I couldn't be teased any more tantalizingly, Jasmine opened one of the bottles of warm oil and poured it directly into the crack of my ass. She paused as the fluid flowed down and directly over my parted lips. I almost came from the gentle movement of the warm liquid as it trickled across the folds of my labia, channeled toward the junction where they joined together at my clit. I shuddered in pleasure at the feeling, even if it was only the subtlest of touch.

Jasmine suddenly interrupted my thoughts.

"Would you like to turn over now?"

It was the first time she had spoken directly to me since the massage started, and it surprised me in my catatonic, pre-orgasmic state. I practically flipped over like a fish out of water and spread my legs expectantly. Finally, I'd get some relief. Surely, she couldn't leave me hanging like this.

"It's time for your final grooming," she said. "I'll need you to part your legs a bit further to provide full access."

Grooming? I knew this was part of the process, but somehow it didn't seem fair to transition at this precise moment. At least I'd be able to stay on the comfortable massage table instead of the clinical vinyl chairs used by my regular esthetician.

Jasmine walked over to another cabinet by the makeup table and withdrew a leather bag from one of the drawers, then brought it back to the table. She reached into the bag and pulled out a cordless hair trimmer.

"Do you have a preference regarding your appearance?" she asked. "Do you prefer natural, neatly trimmed, or bare?"

I knew she was referring to my pubic hair, which I generally kept neatly trimmed. I'd always thought going fully bald was unnatural and unseemly, catering to men's prurient fantasies of fucking young schoolgirls. But in this situation, it seemed entirely appropriate, like I was stripping away all my camouflage and armor.

If tonight was all about being watched, I might as well bare myself in every sense of the word and truly let my inhibitions go. I began to fantasize about rubbing my bare pussy against Jasmine's while she poured warm oil between us. The more work she had to do on me, the more chance I'd have to make this last and hopefully get off.

I didn't hesitate. "Bare, thank you."

"As you wish," she said. "I'll remove the long hairs first with the trimmer, then shave you smooth with a razor."

No waxing? This was different. I was relieved to not have to bear the painful and violent trial of having my hairs ripped out en masse. Although shaving down there was always a scary proposition, I felt safe in the capable and practiced hands of this beautiful esthetician.

Jasmine nodded, then flipped a switch on the trimmer. The

device buzzed softly as she placed it gently on my mound. I had only a light dusting of fur and it didn't take long for her to remove it with a few short strokes over my pubis. I shuddered as the vibrations penetrated deep into my core. If she had placed the flat head on my clitoris, I would have popped off in a millisecond. Instead, she turned the trimmer face-down and gently swiped the vibrating teeth against the sides of my vulva, sensuously separating my labia with her hands as she moved the device between my legs to trim the hairs on the inside and outside of my labia.

It was an insanely titillating feeling, but just clinical enough to bring me down from my plateau and shift my focus. My mind wandered to the upcoming feast, and I contemplated what surprises lay in wait at the main event. The hostesses had suggested there would be 'contact' of some sort during the meal, and I was intrigued exactly who and how it would be administered. The idea of being fully bald, cleansed, and thoroughly stimulated going into the event was an incredible rush.

Jasmine continued with the trimmer all the way down my perineum to my anus, barely touching me with the trimmer so as not to pinch any delicate tissues. Apparently there were no parts of my erogenous zone that would remain untouched, now—and perhaps later.

She turned off the trimmer and placed it at the foot of the table. Then she took a bottle of gel from the bag and spread the gel on her hands. Using both hands, she spread it gently between my legs, starting on my mound all the way down to my rosebud.

My body almost levitated above the table as Jasmine finally laid her hands directly on my clitoris. The gel had a mild stinging quality that added to the stimulating sensation. If this was meant to excite my follicles in preparation for the shave, it wasn't the only feature of my anatomy that it made erect. I could feel the hood of my clitoris retract as my button filled with blood and began to push outward. Suddenly, I was fully stimulated again and lusting for Jasmine's touch. I fantasized about her bending down and taking my swollen nub between her puffy lips and letting me come in her mouth.

Unfortunately, my satisfaction would have to wait a little longer. Instead, Jasmine reached into her bag and pulled out a straight-edge razor. In anyone else's hands, it might look threatening, especially in my prostrated and vulnerable position. But something about the way she delicately and sensuously opened the jackknifed tool instantly evaporated my fears. I could see how this type of razor would in fact give her better control safely cutting my stubs instead of the usual ladies plastic razor.

With her right hand, Jasmine gently laid the razor on its flat edge at the top of my mound, while she gently pulled my skin upwards with her other hand. Then she slowly turned the sharp edge perpendicular to my skin and began softly scraping the razor downwards. I could hear the bristling sound as the razor edge removed my nubs right down to the follicles. She repeated the pattern in one inch wide swipes on one side then the other of my pubis, being ever-so-careful to stop just where my clitoris lay quivering in a mixture of fear and excitement. There was something about the utter vulnerability of the procedure that made it the most erotic experience I'd ever had.

Jasmine used the same deft touch as she moved down my vulva and perineum, scraping the vestiges of stray hairs away with gentle swipes of the long blade, while sensuously separating my folds and flesh with her other hand. She took extra time and care around my anus and clit, using the gentlest and slowest motion I've ever felt someone apply to my body. The combination of fright and titillation as she probed my most sensitive body parts created a river of sensuous fluids running down my vulva. By this time, no shaving gel was necessary to provide a smooth gliding surface for the knife.

When she was finished, Jasmine retrieved a fresh wash towel from beside the sink and held it under the warm water faucet then twisted the excess water into the basin. She returned to the table and placed it over my splayed legs then gently cleansed the excess moisture and remaining shaving gel with gentle massaging movements of her hands. The warm, moist towel felt exquisite against my newly shaved skin. Jasmine's hands now felt comforting between my legs rather than erotic.

She had taken me on an incredibly sensuous erotic arc, right to the edge of ecstasy and back, to a quiet relaxed place. I exhaled fully and completely for the first time in almost an hour.

Jasmine removed the towel from between my legs and held up a large hand mirror at a forty-five degree angle toward me.

"What do you think?" she asked.

I tilted my head up and studied her masterpiece. Far from the usual red and swollen vulva that I typically experienced after the violent waxing with my regular esthetician, I'd never seen my pussy look so beautiful. Utterly bereft of any hair, my entire perineum from my pubic mound to my anus was totally bald, pink—and gorgeous. I just stared at my beautiful pussy, utterly transfixed by the transformation.

"You have to *feel* it to really appreciate how beautiful you are, Jade," Jasmine purred.

I moved my right hand down, running my fingers along the edges of my pussy. I gasped from a feeling I'd never felt before. It felt smooth as silk: no bumps or blemishes or cuts or bruises. It was almost as if I was feeling somebody else—somebody I'd never felt before. I couldn't stop my left hand joining the other in rubbing and caressing my sensitive organs.

Jasmine lowered the mirror and smiled at me as I felt the moisture begin to accumulate between my legs again.

"It's almost time for your dinner appointment," she said. "Why don't you save the best for last? I think you'll find plenty of ways to satisfy your appetite over the next couple of hours."

She lifted my kimono from the hook at the edge of the bathtub and held it open for me.

"I'll escort you downstairs now if you're ready. All you need to bring is your kimono and slippers—and your mask of course."

I sat up slowly and stepped off the massage table. Turning around, I held my arms out as Jasmine lifted one arm of the silk robe onto me then the other. Then she turned around to face me, wrapped the silk tie around me, and tied a single bow over my belly button. She retrieved my matching silk slippers and knelt down on one knee to gently lift my feet one at a time and place them softly inside. It took every ounce of my power not to grab her head and pull it into my pulsating pussy.

Jasmine stood up gracefully and smiled into my eyes.

"If you'll follow me, I'll escort you now to the fantasy feast."

She didn't bother putting her own robe on. Her tight little ass barely jiggled as she stepped smartly ahead of me. I wasn't sure if I'd have a chance to feel Jasmine's touch again before the evening was over, but for now I was in total bliss ogling her petite, curvaceous figure from behind...

Read More

ALSO BY VICTORIA RUSH:

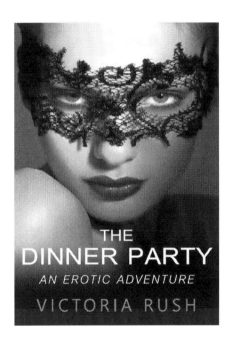

Everyone's an exhibitionist in disguise...

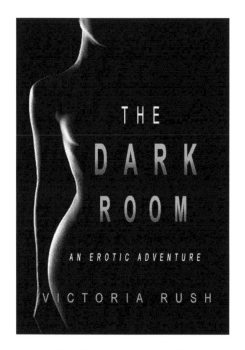

Everything's sexier in the dark...

Printed in Great Britain
by Amazon